The Man Who Dreamed of Elk-Dogs
and Other Stories from the Tipi
© Paul Goble, 2012

Cover: Original painting by Paul Goble

For Janet,
beloved wife
in this world and the next.

Library of Congress Cataloging-in-Publication Data

Goble, Paul.
  The man who dreamed of elk-dogs : and other stories from the tipi / told
and illustrated by Paul Goble ; foreword by Lauren Waukau-Villagomez.
      p. cm.
  Includes bibliographical references and index.
  ISBN 978-1-937786-00-7 (casebound : alk. paper) 1. Indians of North
America--Great Plains--Folklore. 2. Folklore--Great Plains. I. Title.
  E78.G73G673 2012
  398.20978- dc23

                                                                2011051665

Printed in China on acid-free paper
Production Date: 11/21/11
Plant & Location: Printed by Everbest Printing (Guangzhou, China), Co. Ltd
Job / Batch: #105257

Wisdom Tales is an imprint of World Wisdom, Inc.

For information address Wisdom Tales.
P.O. Box 2682, Bloomington, Indiana 47402-2682

www.wisdomtalespress.com

The Man Who Dreamed of Elk-Dogs
& Other Stories from the Tipi

Told and Illustrated by
Paul Goble

Foreword by
Lauren Waukau-Villagomez

Wisdom Tales

Foreword

Over the years, as a professor of children's literature, I used Paul Goble's books when I taught multicultural and Native American literature. Many other teachers have discovered Goble's books to be a valuable resource and have used his stories and pictures in their classrooms.

I corresponded with Paul Goble for a number of years, sharing with him how my sisters and I used his books in our classrooms. In the summer of 2008, my family and I ventured out to Rapid City, South Dakota to meet Paul and his wife for lunch at their home. We were so impressed at what a humble and private person Paul Goble is. After all, he is a Caldecott-winning author. My little niece and nephew were with us on the trip. Paul signed books for them and took pictures with them to share with their classmates in school. It was apparent that Paul is anxious to share his knowledge and stories with his audience, as in no time the children were singing their songs for him and looking at his many picture books.

I have often heard that a wise elder is one who shares the stories of his or her life experiences. Paul Goble, a man who has studied the myths and legends of the Native American people, has clearly learned the wisdom from the stories he has sought to illustrate and retell.

He takes great pride in the fact that his first books were historical fiction told from the Native American perspective (although with some embarrassment because he didn't think they were his best work). My sister, a social studies teacher, uses these books to teach Native American history. Her students can relate to *Red Hawk's Account of Custer's Last Battle*, *Brave Eagle's Account of the Fetterman Fight*, *Lone Bull's Horse Raid*, and *Death of the Iron Horse*.

An issue for many Native Americans is the cultural appropriation of Native stories and who tells our stories. Goble has made a practice of only telling the stories of the Plains Indians as culturally accurate and as close to the oral tradition as possible. Chief Edgar Red Cloud and other Native Americans served as mentors in helping him learn about the culture, history, and mythology. As a result of his study and hard work, his stories and illustrations are culturally correct and significant. His depiction of Native Americans is respectful and fair.

The Man Who Dreamed of Elk-Dogs is an anthology of stories from the Plains Indians, which will make it an excellent reference book in teaching Native stories in the classroom. The stories are representative of all the stories he has collected over the years and Paul includes interesting notes for almost every story. He includes a number of stories about dreams in the book, such as "The Man Who Dreamed of Elk-Dogs," "The Boy Who Saw the All-Wise-One," and "The Mosquitoes," and he discusses in the author's notes the power of dreams for Native people. This certainly resonates for Menominee people because we have been called dreamers with power. Tribes from all over would seek out Menominee people to dream for them.

Although Goble is not Native American, one of my three sisters commented that "he has the heart of a Native American." He is a careful storyteller and has a respect for the authentic voice of the Native people. His interpretation of Native history and legends has held up over and over for more than a generation of readers.

Lauren Waukau-Villagomez
Menominee Indian Reservation

Author's Note

At times most men and women would go alone to a remote place to fast and pray, seeking help and guidance, like the man in this story, "The Man Who Dreamed of Elk-Dogs." Not everyone was rewarded with dreams, but the dreams which were beneficial to all the people were repeated, and their stories became part of the religious beliefs. The story of "The Man Who Dreamed of Elk-Dogs" is one of these, together with others in this collection: "Thunder's Gift of the First Pipe," "The Mosquitoes," "The Doves."

As with the previous two collections, *The Boy and His Mud Horses* and *The Woman Who Lived with Wolves*, I have only chosen the stories which I feel fit comfortably with today's thinking, avoiding stories which involve revenge or killing, and others which need specific knowledge of the culture. Again, the stories are abbreviated; oral tellings would have been much longer.

I have assigned each story to a certain people, Blackfoot, Cheyenne, Lakota, etc., but this is often an arbitrary assignation, reflecting more the recorded version from which I worked. The themes of these stories were often shared across the continent, and I was reminded of this when I was invited to visit Tuscarora students in upstate New York. I had been working on the Blackfoot story of

"The Lost Children," and as it was on my mind, I told them the story. Afterwards their teacher told me that the students were familiar with the story because the Tuscarora tell almost the same story, although separated by half a continent from the Blackfoot.

In the days when Indian peoples told these stories, the world of nature was their whole world. They read it, were in tune with all its aspects, in ways that we can never fully know. We are a frightened people, still living in fear of Mountain Lions, Grizzly Bears, and Wolves; we wage continual warfare on Coyotes, Foxes, Porcupines, Marmots, Bobcats and Prairie Dogs, Raccoons and Skunks, even Squirrels; we dislike Blackbirds and Hawks, Magpies and Crows, and we spray our homes, and poison our surrounds to kill the Mice and Spiders and other insects, even Dandelions and other plants which we designate "noxious weeds." All these need our prayers. In traditional times Indian peoples had no concept of words like *eradicate, exterminate.* Even the humble Doves and Mosquitoes, as told in this collection, had honored places in the peoples' lives and stories. Black Elk, the Lakota holy man, told Joseph Epes Brown in 1950: *One should pay attention to even the smallest crawling creature for these may have a valuable lesson to teach us, and even the smallest ant may wish to communicate with man.*

Blackfoot
The Man Who Dreamed of Elk-Dogs

This story, dear Readers and Listeners, comes from the ancient days when Indian peoples had no horses, just dogs to help them move from one place to another, as they followed the buffalo herds. In those Dog Days tipis were small, because dogs could never drag the long and heavy lodge poles of later Horse Days. In Dog Days people could only have a few possessions; everything had to be carried on their backs or by their dogs. One can only imagine what a blessing horses must have been. As a result, all the stories about the first sight and acquisition of horses are told by the various nations in mythological terms, as gifts from the beneficent spirits. In this story the gift of horses was in answer to a man's prayer and fasting.

In the springtime, when the cottonwood trees had come into leaf and the birds were building nests, a man left the village, feeling the need to fast and pray in the mountains. Wrapped in his blanket and carrying a pipe and tobacco bag, he climbed higher and higher until he was surrounded by a landscape of rocks and snow.

On the fourth night of his fast, when exhausted with hunger, thirst, and cold, he had a dream, and in his dream he saw beautiful animals of many colors, as large as elk, yet as friendly as dogs. A voice spoke: "You will find these animals by a lake far in the north country; they will carry heavier loads than your dogs, and they will make easy the work of men and women. Take a long rope and catch them, and give away all you catch to your people. Go now!"

The man immediately left the mountains, and walked for many days into the far north country until he came to the lake he had seen in his dream. He hid among the bushes at the waters' edge, and there he waited.

Many animals came down to the shore to drink: deer and coyotes, bears and wolves, elk and buffalo, moose and antelope. He waited still, and when he wondered if his dream had been true, a breeze started to blow, and wavelets lapped on the shore, whispering sh-h-h-h-h, sh-h-h-h-h. Emerging from the water were the animals he had seen in his dream, as large as elk but in magnificent colors: blacks, reds, browns, and spotteds, all with beautiful hair trailing on their necks and tails. The man coiled his bull hide rope and caught the tallest and most beautiful of the herd, but the animal pulled and dragged the man about. He could not keep hold, and had to let go. All the animals turned and ran, and disappeared back into the lake; the breeze died, the ripples too.

The man walked back home feeling he had failed; he had not caught the animals he had been shown in his dream. He went again into the high mountains to pray for help. The voice spoke again: "If you fail four times you will never see the animals again. You are not strong enough to hold a big one. Catch a little one."

Feeling encouraged, the man went again to the lake and waited, hidden among the bushes at the edge. Once more he saw many animals come to drink: deer and coyotes, bears and wolves, elk and buffalo, moose and antelope. And then, once more, the breeze started to blow, and ripples to break on the shore, whispering sh-

The dark one with the big ears is a mule.

Two handsome stallions.

h-h-h-h, sh-h-h-h-h. The beautiful animals came to the shore: blacks, reds, browns, and spotteds. The man coiled his bull-hide rope, and caught a young one which he held easily.

The days passed, and when he had caught all the young ones, he set out to return to his village. He had not gone far, when all the mother animals trotted after them; their udders filled with milk.

At first the people were afraid of the strange animals, which were as strong and tall as elk, but very soon the men were mounting the animals and chasing the buffalo. The women put packs on the animals' backs, and made them drag their lodge poles, just as their dogs had always done. They called these new and beautiful animals, Elk-Dogs.

Can you imagine, dear Readers and Listeners, how proud the man must have been to bring home all those horses? So proud, indeed, that I have painted the scene as he might have painted it, because all men liked to keep a picture record of such special events. I have taken elements from another Native American painting (Lakota), which pictures bringing horses home. I have carefully copied the drawing of the horses, but I have added color which the painter would surely have used, had such colors been available in the 1860s. Note the ingenious way the painter drew the horses; note all those legs, and even some he forgot!

The man with his rope, and his hair in a topknot style.

Missing legs!

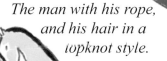

Lakota

The Man Who Shot a Ghost

No book of stories is complete without a ghost story. Here is one which has come down to us from Buffalo Days.

A man went hunting, but when evening approached he was a long way from home. He made a fire and went to sleep hungry, as he had found no food that day.

In the middle of the night he awoke hearing a woman wailing: "My Son! My Son!" again and again, "My Son! My Son!" He quickly made up the fire for more light. Then he covered himself with his blanket, and tore a hole just large enough to peep through. He lay there, holding his flintlock gun, ready for anything.

Soon he heard twigs breaking under the feet of someone approaching. He peeped through the hole in his blanket, hardly daring to breathe. It was a woman, snuffling as she came, her robe pulled over her head, wearing a buckskin dress and leggings with embroidered designs. She stood by him a while, and then ever so slowly, lifted up one of his feet. When she let it go, he let it fall with a thud as if he were dead. She raised it a second time, and then a third, and still the man never moved. The woman then pulled a large rusty knife from her belt, and suddenly seizing his foot was about to gash it when the man sprung up yelling: "What are you doing?" Not waiting for an answer, he fired his gun and the woman fled, screaming, "Yun! yun! yun! yun! yun!" vanishing into the night.

The man reloaded his gun, and again hid under his blanket, but he never slept. When it grew light he saw that he had been sleeping close to an old burial scaffold, its bones only half covered with tattered and torn blankets and robes.

You may have wondered, dear Readers and Listeners, why there is no illustration here. The illustrator of these pages said he didn't like to paint ghosts, but in truth he lacked the skill. . .

Lakota
The Grateful Wolf

A man found a wolf's den. He could hear the cubs inside talking. Thinking to take the cubs home for his children, he started to dig them out. The mother wolf was close by and came running, "Have pity on my children," she barked. When the man took no notice, she called her husband, and he, too, came running. He sang a song: "O Man, if you will have pity on our children, I will help you greatly with my power." He howled and a mist descended; he howled again, and the mist lifted just as suddenly.

"This wolf has wonderful powers," the man thought to himself. When he had dug down to the cubs, he tore strips from his red blanket, and lifting out the cubs, he tied a strip around each cub's neck, like a necklace. He used sacred red paint to paint their noses and paws, and then he put them back in their den. The grateful father wolf told the man: "When you go next to capture horses from your enemies, I will go with you, and help you."

In time the man left the village to capture horses, and the wolf went with him. When they approached the enemy village, the wolf said: "I will sing, and you will steal their horses, and they will never know." The wolf howled, and a great wind arose, and the horses fled to the shelter of the trees. The wolf howled again; the wind died, and a fog arose. The man took as many horses as he could drive home.

In gratitude the man promised that whenever he brought home food for his family, he would always leave some food outside the camp circle for the wolves.

The Woman Married to a Horse

It was springtime, and the dried meat in the rawhide cases was almost all eaten. Everyone needed fresh meat, but the buffalo herds had not yet returned. The elders told two young men, known to be reliable, to climb a distant butte, and to look for the herds.

The young men did not see any buffalo, but far off in the distance, they were greatly surprised to see what appeared to be a person running with a herd of wild horses. As they watched, they saw that it was a woman with long hair streaming out behind her as she ran. "This is very strange," one said to the other. "We must go back and tell the elders."

They described what they had seen, and asked whether a woman had ever been missing. "Yes," answered an old man. "I remember years ago, not so far from here, a man lost his young wife. She was never found. This must be her. We must bring her home."

The men caught their fastest horses and rode out to surround the wild horses. The woman was as wild as the horses and difficult to catch, but they roped her by an arm and a leg. To stop her struggles they picketed her together with the other wild horses.

That night a young man left his tipi and laid down beside her. She spoke to him: "Listen to me, young man, for I tell you the truth: it was many years ago when the village was moving. I was lagging behind everyone a little, when I saw a beautiful black stallion with a rope on him. I thought he must belong to someone in the village. When I had hold of his rope, he suddenly spoke to me: 'Jump on my back.' He took me away. He is my husband," she said, pointing to a black stallion picketed close by. "And those are my seven children," she said, pointing them out. "I cannot go back to this village life now. I have become a horse. Let me and my children go. If you help me, then I will help you: tie a bell to your horse, you will always be lucky at catching wild horses."

The young man told the elders what the woman had told him. After considering among themselves, the elders cried out to the people to set free the woman and the wild horses.

They say this happened in the long-ago times, when all things were possible.

Blackfoot
The Mosquitoes

Every nation had societies of men who policed the good order of the people. The chiefs and elders could call upon one of the societies to organize the buffalo hunt so that everyone benefited, or to ensure proper discipline when the people moved from one place to another, even to distribute food fairly at a time of scarcity. All men were members of one society or another, usually according to age. Among the Blackfoot people there were the Doves for older boys (see opposite page), the Mosquitoes for young men, Braves for grownups, and Mad Dogs for older men. This story is how the young men's Mosquitoes Society originated.

Once when hunting, a man found himself in a place where there were swarms of mosquitoes. They attacked him so hungrily that he imagined they were starving. He took off his clothes and lay down. The hungry mosquitoes covered his body, biting him in every part until he lost all feeling. He dreamed he heard singing:

> *Mosquitoes, mosquitoes,*
> *Get together, get together,*
> *Mosquitoes get together.*
> *Our friend is nearly dead!*

It was the mosquitoes in a circle; jumping up and down, each facing the sun. Some were painted red, others yellow, and all had eagle claws attached to their wrists and long plumes hanging from the backs of their heads. And then he heard a voice saying: "Brother, because you let us drink from your body, we make you, the leader of the Mosquitoes Society among your people."

The man went home and started the Mosquitoes Society. At meetings some painted themselves red, others yellow, and each wore a long plume. When they danced they waved their buffalo robes like wings, and made a high-pitched buzzing which mosquitoes make. At the close of their dance they would chase people, even into their tipis like mosquitoes, and would scratch them with their eagle claws. Those who offered no resistance, were left alone.

The story reminds me that one evening as the light was fading, I found Tom Yellowtail, Holy Man of the Crow Nation, working in his vegetable garden, close to the Little Bighorn River. It was the time when the breezes vanish and the mosquitoes wake up. Tom stopped his work, lent on his spade and talked, and when Tom talked, he talked slowly, and at great length. There was I, standing, listening, being eaten alive by mosquitoes, simply dying to swat them here, there, and everywhere, whereas Tom never showed he even noticed them. With that example, how could a white man be so wimpish as to show that he noticed the pesky mosquitoes?

Blackfoot
The Doves

There was an old man who loved his grandson, but when the grandson died, the old man left the village and went far away from people into the mountains to cry. It was in the fall of the year, the time when the Doves like to gather together. They joined the old man in his sadness, coo-cooing mournfully with him. But they told him not to cry, and that when he got home again to start the Doves Society for all the other boys his beloved grandson had known.

Blackfoot
The Wolf-Man

There was a man who had two wives; they were sisters, but they were not good wives. They had no shame. Hoping to teach them better ways, he moved his lodge away from the village, far out on the prairies. They set up camp beneath a high butte, and every evening the man climbed to the top to look out over the plains to see where the buffalo herds were grazing. He would sit on a buffalo skull until it was almost dark, when he would return to his lodge.

The wives grumbled to each other: "This is a lonely life with nobody to talk to, no excitement." "Yes," the other said, "so let's kill our husband. Then we can go home, and have a good time again."

One morning when the man had gone hunting, the sisters went to the top of the butte, and dug a deep pit. They covered it over with slender twigs and grass, and placed the buffalo skull on top. That evening, as was his custom, the man climbed the butte, and sitting upon the buffalo skull, he fell down into the pit. When the sisters saw him disappear, they took down the lodge and headed for home. Next morning as they approached within earshot of the village, they started to cry and mourn; "Our beloved husband is dead. He went away to hunt, but never returned." They cried and cried.

The man was badly hurt, and could not climb out of the pit. A wolf found him. "Ah-wh-o-o-o-o! Come! See what I have found," he howled, and many other wolves came, and with them, coyotes, badgers, and foxes as well. "We must get him out of here," the wolf said. "As it was I who found him, he will be my brother, and I, and my wolf brothers, will look after him," and all the animals thought that was a good plan. The wolves took him to their home, where an old blind wolf with mystic powers made him better.

The man loved his wolf brothers. He taught them to avoid the traps and snares which men laid to kill them. People became suspicious: "It must be a man-wolf who knows how to spring our traps and draw our snares," they said. "We must catch him." They laid out their very best food as bait, pemmican and buffalo back fat, and then they waited, hidden, close by. When the man saw such good food, he ate eagerly, having not eaten real food for so long. People rushed out from their hiding places and captured him. "Look! This is the man who never returned from hunting!" they exclaimed in surprise. "No!" the man told them. "My wives tried to kill me. They dug a deep hole, in which I fell, and was badly hurt. My wolf brothers took pity on me, or I would have died."

The women vanished, never to be seen again in the village.

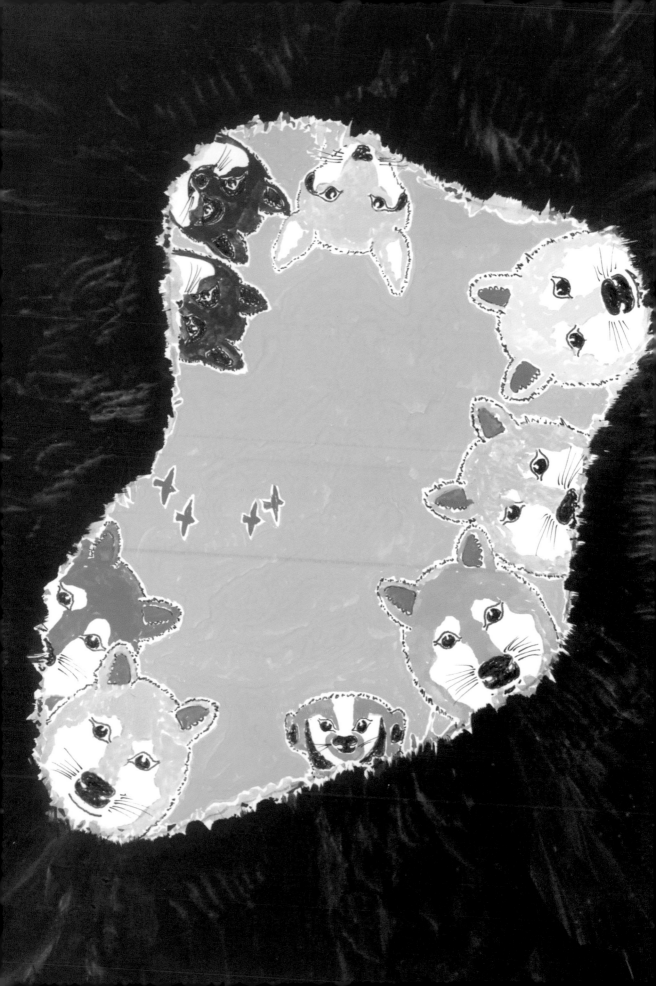

Blackfoot and Many Nations
The Wicked Raven

Many of these stories are from the Cheyenne and Blackfoot peoples, recorded by George Bird Grinnell from men and women who had grown up and lived during Buffalo Days.

"The Wicked Raven" is another recorded by Grinnell. The story tells of the times before the introduction of horses, when people killed herds of buffalo by a combination of driving over cliffs, and enticement into box-canyons or enclosures. Much depended upon the knowledge and skill , and the sacred power, of the man who led the hunt, the Buffalo Caller as he was known. He is a powerful and truly mysterious figure in ancient Plains Indian life. Disguised as a buffalo, he would leave the village, usually for several days, patiently drawing the buffalo herds into the traps where everyone waited to kill them. He had developed a special relationship with the buffalo; he could lead them because he loved them, and

understood their thoughts and fears and curiosities. It was diffi-cult and dangerous work which relied upon the cooperation of the entire community for a successful kill. Even a dog barking at the last moment, a child playing, or a raven calling could upset all the plans, and the buffalo herd would shy away avoiding the trap.

One day, not long after *Napi*, Old Man, had finished his work of creation, he heard the people calling: "*Napi*, we are hungry, save us or we will die." Every time the people drove the buffalo to the edge of the cliff, Raven would swoop down in front of the leading buffaloes and the herd would turn off to one side. "It's a trap! Save yourselves!" Raven screamed at the top of his voice, and the buffa-loes would escape the trap, and the people would still be hungry.

Napi saw how it was and changing himself into a dead beaver, he lay down beside the river. It was not long before hungry Raven flew down and started to peck at him. *Napi* caught him by his legs and took him to the village where the elders debated what should be done with him. "Pull out his feathers! Cut out his tongue!" some said; "Kill him!" said others. But *Napi* said: "No! We will punish him," and he tied him by his legs to the top of the lodge, and there Raven had to stay day after day in the smoke of the cook-ing fire below. His eyes clouded over, and his once loud voice be-came hoarse until all he could say was a low, deep "Croak!"

Napi untied him and told him: "Never try to fool me! Look at me! Don't you know that I am *Napi*! I made you! I made these great plains. I made the mountains. I am all powerful! Go back to your wife and your children, and behave yourself in future."

The Boy Who Saw the All-Wise-One

The Pawnee people had wandered, walking for more days than they could remember, always weaker and weaker with hunger, searching for the buffalo herds. They had eaten their last corn and dried meat, and were eating their robes and moccasins. Babies were dying, Even the dogs were too weak to drag their loads. The people had reached the end; they could go no farther.

There was a poor orphan boy who lived with a kindly old lady. He suffered like everyone else, and thought to himself: "This is where I will die," and he lay down beside the fire to keep warm. Whether waking or fainting, we do not know, but he could see, between himself and the sun, two birds flying toward him, coming closer and closer. They were swans, and they landed, one either side of him. Lifting the boy with their wings, they flew with him on their backs, and put him down again in front of a tipi. It was the tallest and most beautiful tipi the boy had ever seen, painted with birds and animals in many colors.

The All-Wise-One was sitting at the back, and round the lodge were seated many important people wearing the finest clothes. "Welcome, my son," the All-Wise-One greeted him, and to one of the men he said, "Give this boy something to eat." He was given only a small piece of dried meat, and he wondered why the man gave such a little piece, but as he ate, the piece remained the same size in his mouth, and soon he was no longer hungry.

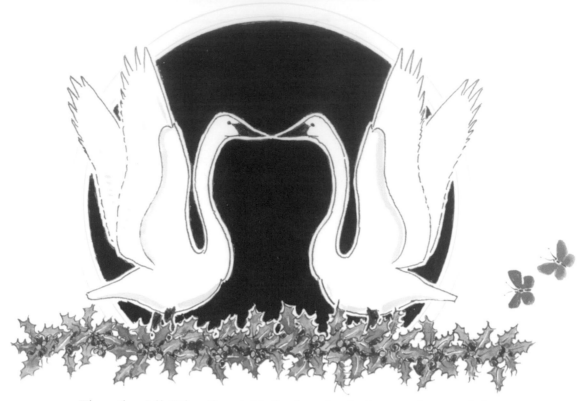

Then the All-Wise-One told the boy he had seen the people's suffering, and was sorry for them, and he explained to the boy how he would help his people when he returned home. He gave him beautiful clothes and led him outside the lodge to where the swans were waiting to take him home.

Who can tell whether the boy was awake, or asleep? The fire had gone out, but he stood up and went outside, feeling strong once more. The old lady was amazed to see him in his new clothes, and looking so strong and well. When the boy entered the lodge again, he saw that she was preparing to cook the last piece of robe, but he told her: "Leave that. Go out and bring in some meat." The woman was mystified, but she did as he told, and by the lodge door there was a pile of fresh meat. Soon she had cooked enough to satisfy everyone in the village. Afterwards the pipes were lighted, and the people gave thanks: "Father, All-Wise-One, you are the ruler," the old men said.

The boy told a young man: "Run hard to the top of that hill, and tell me what you see." When the young man reached the top, he could see nothing more than the prairie and buttes. The boy told him to try again, harder. When the young man failed to see anything a third time, the boy, himself, ran to the top, and looking toward the south, the prairie was black with herds of grazing buffalo. He waved his robe, signaling to the village that he had seen buffalo. Immediately the men grabbed their bows and arrows, and joined the boy on the hilltop.

Winnebago
Mouse Chief

There were several families of mice who lived underneath a fallen tree. They had never seen anyone else, and believed they were the only people in the world. When Mouse Chief stood on his toes and stretched up his arms he could just reach the underside of the fallen tree. He believed himself to be tall enough to even touch the sky. He was so happy that he danced, and sang:

> *There is nobody like me!*
> *Nobody anywhere like me!*
> *I can touch the sky!*
> *Yes! I can touch the sky!*

Omaha
The Bird Chief

In was in the Beginning Times, they say, that all the birds came together to decide who would be their chief. They decided that whoever could fly the highest would be chief.

All the birds set off with a great whirring of wings. Crow and Hawk took the lead, leaving the small birds behind, but everyone knew it would be a contest between Eagle and Vulture. They were always flying the highest, making circles, watching what goes on down below. But nobody knew, not even Eagle, that tiny Wren had tucked himself underneath the feathers on Eagle's back.

When all the birds had come back down, exhausted, Eagle and Vulture were still flying higher, circling, always circling. Finally Vulture was tired and circled back down. Eagle flew a little higher, before following Vulture. Just at that moment, Wren, fresh from the ride, flew high up, higher still than Eagle.

When Eagle had come back down, all the birds were agreed that he would be chief. But then they heard a clear trilling voice, high, high up. It was Wren, so high that nobody could see him. He had flown the highest. Little Wren with the big voice was made chief.

Blackfoot
Thunder's Gift of the First Pipe

Long ago, all-powerful Thunder struck the lodge of a young man and his wife. At first, neighbors thought the young man was dead, but he soon recovered. He could not find his wife, and he soon realized she had not just gone to fetch water or wood, but was nowhere to be found! People said that Thunder must surely have stolen her. . . .

The man was overcome with grief. He left the village, not knowing which way to go. He asked the birds and animals if they knew where Thunder lived, but they were too afraid to talk. "Go home!" Wolf told him. "When Thunder strikes, we are dead."

But still the young man walked on, until high in the mountains he came to a lodge made of stone, which belonged to the Raven chief. "Welcome, friend," he said. "Why have you come?" The young man told how he was looking for his wife, and he covered his head with his robe and cried. Raven told him: "Thunder lives close by, in a stone lodge like this. But nobody dares to enter. Hanging on the walls are the eyes of the people he has killed. Yes! It's a dreadful place! No man can enter and live. There is just one that Thunder fears, and cannot kill, and that is I, chief of all the Ravens. Take this Raven's wing; point it at him and he cannot harm you, and this elk-horn arrow too. Go! Search for your wife's eyes! The wing and arrow will protect you."

Entering Thunder's lodge, the young man sat close by the doorway. In the gloom at the back, sat dreaded Thunder, watching with malevolent piercing eyes. "You dare to enter my lodge," roared Thunder. "No man comes here and lives," and as he rose to strike, the man pointed the Raven's wing, and Thunder fell back. He rose again, and the young man shot the elk-horn arrow through the lodge cover, and suddenly sunlight filled that gloomy place. "Stop!" cried Thunder. "You are stronger! Take your wife's eyes, and have her back." The man cut the string which held them, and at that instant his beloved wife was beside him again.

Thunder spoke again: "Everyone knows my power! Everyone fears me! I live here during the summer, but when winter comes I travel with the birds far to the south." And then Thunder gave the man a bundle. "Take this pipe to your people. When you hear me return in the springtime, unwrap the pipe, and pray for my protection. I'll see the rising smoke, and I'll bring the rains to make everything grow, and to fill the berries with juice."

So it was that a young man, when searching for his wife, also received the first sacred pipe for his people.

Lakota

The Raccoon and the Crayfish

There was little to eat in the Crayfish village. The children were crying with hunger. The elders sent out a young one to walk along the stream to look for something to eat. Raccoon caught sight of him and planned to catch him: lying down beside the stream, he pretended to be dead.

Soon Crayfish came upon him. "Wow! Here's something to eat! But is it dead? I'll pinch its nose with my claws and find out," and he tweaked Raccoon's nose, but Raccoon never moved. He pinched and tickled Raccoon's ribs until Raccoon could hardly stop from laughing. "He's dead," Crayfish said to himself, and he went home to tell what he had found.

The Crayfishes left their village and marched along the river in single file, chiefs first, followed by the men, then the women and children, and the old people taking up the rear. They formed a circle round Raccoon and danced and sang:

> *We'll have a great feast!*
> *Spotted Face is dead.*
> *We'll have a great feast!*
> *We'll dance and celebrate!*

As they danced, Raccoon suddenly stood up. "Who did you say you were going to eat? Me? You call me Spotted Face? Watch me: I'll crunch up all your claws, backs, legs, everything," and Raccoon rushed among them. The Crayfishes never feasted on Raccoon; Raccoon feasted on them!

Hidatsa

The Forgotten One

Once a woman went to her garden to harvest the last of the corn for her family to eat during the winter. When she had torn the last ear from the stalks, and her basket was full, she was leaving her garden to return home when she heard a child crying: "Please don't go! Don't leave me!"

The woman was astonished. "Can there really be a child here?" she wondered. She looked all round but seeing nothing, she started on her way again. "Please, please don't leave me!" again the child cried. The woman was mystified. There was no child anywhere. She was taking up her basket again, when the voice cried a third time: "Please don't leave me behind!"

The woman put down her basket and searched thoroughly among the stalks throughout the garden, and hidden among the yellow leaves she found a small ear of corn. This was the voice she had heard, and never wasteful, she added the forgotten one to her basket.

Little stories like these, dear Readers and Listeners, were told to children. Each contained a moral, which was not explained, but was left for children to think about.

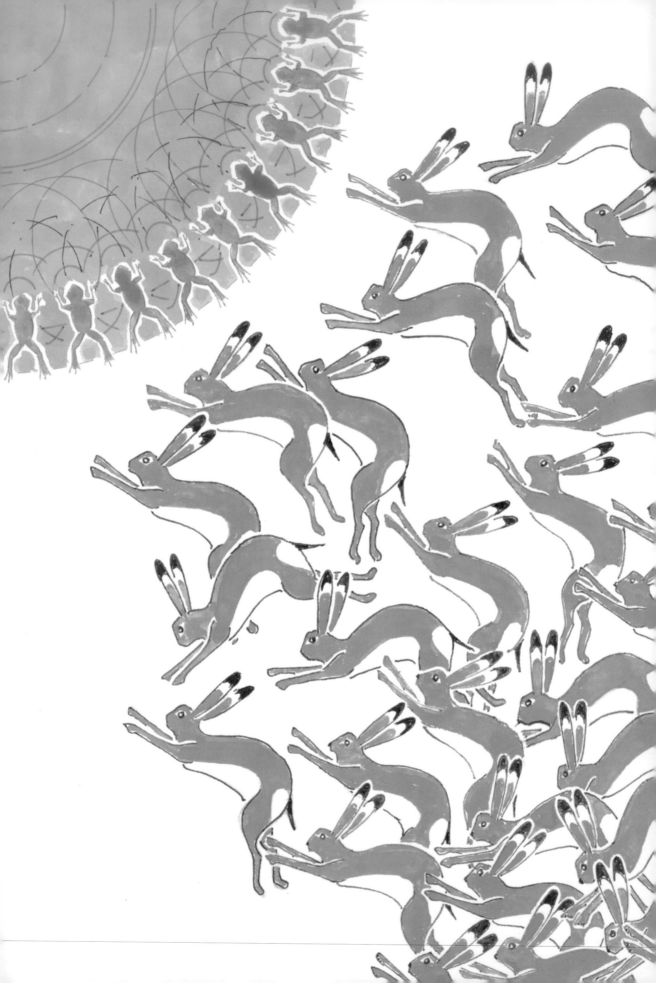

Lakota

The Rabbits' Resolution

On one level this story is for the little children, told here in a modern way. Unlike Aesop, Indian people do not point out the moral of a story; instead it is there for you, dear Readers and Listeners, to think about for yourselves. The Rabbits in this story are the large long-eared Jackrabbits, or Hares, of the semi-arid Great Plains, not the little Cottontails.

All the Rabbits were depressed. Yes, it seemed that everyone was against them. They had to watch the sky for Hawks and Eagles, and they had to constantly keep an eye open for Wolves, Coyotes, and Foxes, even Weasels and Ferrets, and Otters as well, because it was hardly safe for Rabbits to drink at the river. They had no way to defend themselves, except to run and hide down their burrows, and then to wait, and wait, until it was safe to come out again. The whole world was against them. It was no way to live, and so who can wonder they were depressed?

One day, long ago, all the Rabbits came together for a big meeting. For days they talked about their experiences, one sad story after another about how a parent or grandparent, a son or daughter, had been killed, and then, worse still, *eaten*. . . . It could not go on.

Finally the chiefs and elders came to a decision: "Ladies and Gentlemen, we Rabbits are a sorry lot. We are pushed around by everyone. Nobody likes us. Nobody gives us respect. Everyone hates us. We cannot defend ourselves. It would be far better we had never been born. There is nothing else for it: we must all go down to the lake and drown ourselves."

And that is what they decided. Running down to the lake and about to jump in, *plop! plop! plop! plop!* a lot of Frogs jumped into the water in front of the Rabbits.

"Stop! Hold it!" cried the chiefs. "No, we'll not drown ourselves! Forget it! Here's people even more timid than us: the Frog Nation!"

Pawnee
The Spirit Wife

Life and death are the great mysteries, in which we seek to find meaning. All peoples, ever since the world began, have wondered, and like the Pawnee people in this story, they have told how it is.
There was a young man in the village who was in deepest mourning for his wife. Day after day he would take his little boy, and they would go and sit beneath the scaffold on which her blanket--wrapped body rested. There they cried, lost with sadness that she was no longer with them. "Mother, come back home," the little boy wept, "I want you," and his father, too, cried with loneliness.

One time the young man fell asleep, tired out with sadness. It was after dark when he awoke to find someone standing over him. It was his beloved wife! "I see you are both so sad," she said. "I have come to tell you that where I have been there is no unhappiness, nothing bad. You and our little boy must come there with me." But the young man did not want to die. "No, please come back to us, and we will all be happy here once again."

Then the woman agreed to come back, "but the curtain must remain drawn shut around my bed for four days. Nobody must look behind it," and the young man told her that nobody would look. When the four days had passed, his young wife came out from behind the curtain. Her relations came to see, and then all the people came, and everybody was glad she had come back.

After some years had passed, the man took a second wife. This new wife was often bad-tempered and always quarrelsome, and was jealous of the first wife. One day she said to the first wife: "You shouldn't even be here; go back to wherever you came from! You're nothing but a spirit anyway!"

That night, as always, the man lay down with his first wife, but when he awoke in the morning, she was no longer beside him. The following night the man and the boy both died in their sleep. The woman had called them to herself. And that, they say, is how Pawnee people know there is another life after this.

Let's see, is this real,
Let's see, is this real.
This life I am living?
You spirits, everywhere,
Let's see, is this real,
This life I am living?

Pawnee warrior's song.

Blackfoot

The Puppy and the Digging Stick

Every day the hunters returned empty handed; the buffalo were no-where to be found. Everyone was hungry. They prayed: "Oh *Napi*, Creator, help us, or we die."

Napi heard their prayers, and taking a young man from the village, they set out to find the buffalo. After days walking, they came to a lodge by a river. *Napi* told the young man: "This is where the man lives who has hidden the buffaloes. He has a wife and little boy."

As they approached, Almighty *Napi* turned himself into a puppy, and the young man into a digging stick. When the little boy saw the puppy, he hugged it and told his father: "Look what a lovely puppy I have found." But his father told him: "Throw it away; it's not a puppy." The boy cried, but when he found the digging stick, he ran to his mother. "Look, Mother, at this pretty digging stick!" "Throw it away!" the father ordered. "It's not a digging stick," but his wife answered: "No! I want to have it, and let our boy have the puppy." "Have it your way," the man answered, "but if trouble comes, it will be your fault."

The next morning the boy and his mother took the stick to dig roots, and the puppy followed. They came to a cave with a buffalo cow standing at the entrance. Immediately the puppy ran inside and the stick slipped from the woman's hands and followed, slithering along like a snake. Inside the cave were all the buffaloes, and they began driving them out.

The man came running, "Who is driving out my buffaloes?" he cried, and the woman answered, "The dog and the stick went inside." The man was angry: "I told you they were not what they seemed? Look what you have done!" He fitted an arrow to his bow and waited for the puppy and the stick to appear. But when the last big bull was about to leave, the stick twisted itself among the hair under the bull's chin, and the puppy grabbed the long hair underneath. The man never saw them leave the cave.

Once again the prairie was covered with herds of buffalo.

Cheyenne
Saved by Their Dogs

Many of these old stories tell of times when people could not find the buffalo herds upon which they depended for food and all their needs. In those ancient days they had no horses, only dogs to help them carry their tipis and belongings. The people walked in search of the herds; they walked, carrying their children on their backs; sometimes they walked until they and their dogs were too weak with hunger to go any farther, and then the people starved. No wonder such terrible times were remembered. . . .

The leaders decided that the women and children were too weak to walk any farther, and even the dogs were starving, and could hardly be urged to carry their burdens any farther. Young men, who still had strength enough, were sent out in every direction to look for the buffalo herds, while the people pitched the tipis beside a river. There was nothing more to eat; the rawhide cases, which had been filled with dried meat, were empty.

The leaders ordered that every day each family should kill and eat one of its dogs. Even though he was as hungry as everyone else, there was a boy who loved his dog more than anything else. He could not bare the thought of it being killed. Each day he feared it would be next. He told the dog: "Go and hide. Find a safe place. Take all the dogs with you, and don't come back or they will surely kill you all. Go quickly." When people awoke next morning there was not a dog in the camp.

The next night the boy had a dream: he dreamed that the dogs had been hunting and had plenty of meat. He dreamed that his dog brought him a piece, and told him: "I will take you to where we have meat for everyone, but people must first promise never again to eat dogs, except for important occasions." In his dream, his dog repeated the same thing four times: "People must never again eat dogs, except for special occasions."

When he awoke, there was a piece of meat by his bed, and on the dirt floor of the tipi, the footprints of his beloved dog. The boy gave the meat to his mother. Then he told everyone about his dream, and they followed his dog's footprints until they came to where the dogs were hiding. Each dog sat beside a pile of meat for his family. "Remember," the boy reminded the people, "we will never again eat dogs, except for special occasions."

And that is how it was in ancient times, dear Readers and Listeners, and if you had been favored as a specially honored guest, your host might have sacrificed one of his small puppies in your honor. To have refused to eat would have been the height of bad manners!

The Beginning of Death

Napi, Old Man, the Creator, made the world as we see it today: the mountains and rivers, the great plains and forests, and he made the birds and animals, the fishes and insects. Everything.

One day Old Man decided to make a woman and child. He formed them out of red clay, telling the clay, "You will be a woman and her child." He covered them with cottonwood leaves and left them to dry. The next morning he peeped under the leaves, but the clay was still wet, and it was the same the next day. On the fourth day he pulled the leaves away, and told them: "My name is *Napi*, Old Man, and I am your Maker. Stand up now and follow me," and he took them down to the river to drink.

While standing by the river, the woman asked him: "Will we die, or will we live forever?" Old Man thought for a moment and answered: "I'll throw this buffalo chip into the water. If it floats, people will die for four days and live again, but if it sinks they'll die forever." He threw the buffalo chip into the water, and it floated. "No!" said the woman. "I will throw this stone into the water. If it floats we will always live, but if it sinks we will die." She threw the stone into the water, and it sank. "Okay," said Old Man, "you have chosen. People will die, but their friends and relatives will be sad that they are no longer living."

A few days later the woman's child died, and she went to *Napi* crying: "Please let us have death as you said it should be, and then my beloved child will come back to me again in four days." "No," said *Napi*, "what was decided, was decided. We will undo nothing. The child is dead, and that is that. People will have to die forever, but you will always remember your child."

That is how we came to be people. It is *Napi*, Old Man, the Creator, who made us.

This is only one part of the story of Creation. In the oral tradition there is a story about how almost everything came into being: fire for cooking, tipis for shelter, hunting, why animals and birds live where they do, how the hills and mountains were shaped. Important, too, is the story of how people received bows and arrows, because in the early times, they say, buffalo used to eat people, and the proof is the long hair on the buffalo's chin, the hair of the people he used to eat. With bows and arrows people no longer lived in fear of the buffalo. Stories of Creation were as many as the storyteller's imagination and memory.

Cheyenne

Sees in the Night

The people were on the move, following the buffalo herds. When they came to a wide river, the leaders said that everyone should cross over and set up the tipis on the far side.

There was a boy who crossed after everyone else. The day was hot, and on the far side of the river he lay down in the shade of an old oak tree and went to sleep. He was poor, an orphan, living here one day, somewhere else the next, always hungry, having to beg for something to eat.

In his sleep the boy heard a dog singing. He could not hear the words, but the voice was like that of a young woman. The song was repeated, and after each, the dog howled four times like a wolf. The dog came closer, singing, and now the boy could hear the words, "Boy, take pity on my children. Carry them across this river. I know you are a poor boy, and have no father, no home. If you take my children safely across the river, I will help you."

The boy awoke to see the dog and and her puppies on the far side. He waded across and took two of the puppies across. He went back and carried two more, and when he carried the last, the mother dog swam across beside him.

And then she spoke, "Boy, I know you have no name, no home, no relations, no friends. Look at your robe, all tattered and torn, and your moccasins full of holes. But when you grow up all this will change, if you do what I tell you. Whenever a party of men leave to capture horses from our enemies, you must wait two or three days, and then follow after them. Leave at night, and you will be able to follow their trail, because night will be to you just the same as day. People will come to call you Sees in the Night. You will capture many horses and be rich; you will marry and have friends and relations. Remember what I say!"

The boy never told anyone what the dog promised, and later when he was a young man he would go out into the hills at night to pray for help to understand, and to be worthy of the promise the dog had given.

To be able to see at night would have given the young man the ability to go into the enemy camps at night and to take out the favorite horses picketed close to their owners' tipis. He would soon have developed a reputation for success, and other young men would have sought his leadership. To capture horses, and then to give them away, demonstrated bravery, both in the enemy camps, and the act of generosity itself. He would have become a sought-after son-in-law, and married, and gained friends and relations. All these things the mother dog foretold.

Cheyenne
The Little Girl and the Ghoul

One evening a little girl would not stop crying. Perhaps she was cross about something. Her mother tried everything to stop her tears, but finally, quite out of patience, she announced: "Ghoul, take this child!" and she pushed the child outside the tipi into the darkness.

It happened that at that very moment a Ghoul was close by, and it snatched up the little girl. When her mother heard no more crying, she went outside to bring her daughter in, but she could not find her. It was the same when daylight came; nobody saw the child again.

The Ghoul took the girl to its tipi. "Go and bring me firewood!" it ordered. While she was picking up pieces of wood, a little bird spoke to her: "You are gathering that wood, because the Ghoul means to eat you." When the girl returned to the tipi with her load, the Ghoul was angry. "No! Not cottonwood! Bring me willow-wood." When she brought willowwood, the Ghoul demanded ashwood, and a fourth time, birchwood.

As she worked the little bird spoke again: "This is the last time. Now the Ghoul will kill you." "But there is nothing I can do," the girl replied. "The Ghoul has me in its power. Help me!" The little bird told her: "I will take you to the mountain where Thunder lives. He will protect you. There is a door to his lodge among the rocks. But before he will open it, you have to say: 'My Grandfather, I have come for help; my Father, I have come for help; my Brother, I have come for help.'"

Then the little bird told the girl to hold on to his back, and he carried her to the top of the mountain. The girl repeated the words which the bird had told her; and the rock door slid aside. Thunder was sitting inside. "Come in, my Grandchild," he said. "I know you have come to me for protection."

Meanwhile the Ghoul saw where the girl had gone, and followed, all the while hooting like an owl, so loud that the mountain shook. "Bring out my meat," it screamed, "or I will come in and get it!" The little girl ran around inside the lodge, looking for somewhere to hide, but Thunder told her not to be afraid. "Bring out my meat! Bring out my meat!" the Ghoul shrieked again and again. "Come in and take it," Thunder answered, and he opened the door a little. As the Ghoul put its head inside, the door closed with a flash of lightning, cutting off its head.

Thunder threw the head outside and told the little girl to build a fire and to burn the Ghoul. "If anything rolls out of the fire, don't touch it; push it back," and he gave her a stick. Soon the Ghoul's body cracked open in the heat and shiny, brightly colored beads and fine flint arrowheads popped out. The girl wanted to play with them, but Thunder told her to push them back, and soon the Ghoul's body was just ashes.

The girl lived in the protection of Thunder's lodge until she was seventeen years old, when he told her it was time for her to return to her people. He made clothes for her: a buffalo robe, moccasins, and leggings, all of which he painted red.

When she came to the camp of her people, nobody recognized her. "This is my home," she told them. "I have been away for many years." But still nobody knew her. She was ashamed to have to tell that she was the little girl who had cried, and had been pushed outside the tipi, and snatched by a Ghoul. Then people remembered, and her family were glad to take her home again.

Thunder, dear Readers and Listeners, protects the purity of little children from horrible ghouls, and he even protects them from their own temptations, here, playing with pretty beads. Thunder's power is truly awesome, yet he also brings the rain to give us life.

Blackfoot
The Horse Lodge

Blackfoot people prefer to use the word lodge rather than tipi. This story tells of an old Black Mare, but I have to tell you, dear Readers and Listeners, that the original story told of a White Mare, but the illustrator found it difficult to paint a white horse . . . and, searching the museum photographic archives of the late 1800s and early 1900s, Horse Lodges had painted black *horses.*

During Buffalo Days a man who had many horses was wealthy. He could lend horses to those who had none to hunt buffalo, in return for meat or hides. With many horses he could carry a large lodge, even more than one, but mostly he wanted horses to give away; a generous man was a brave man, and was looked to as a leader and provider. Generosity was one of the four virtues people strived for in life: Kindness, Patience, Wisdom, and Generosity.

There was a poor young man in the village who had only one horse, an old Black Mare which he loved more than anything. In time he captured horses from his enemies, and collected together a very considerable herd, but he still loved his Black Mare best. He looked after her well, never making her work. He was surprised when she gave birth to a beautiful black colt.

One day when he took the Black Mare and her colt down to the river to drink, she suddenly spoke to him: "Father, I want to give you something important," she told him. "Tomorrow when you go out to the meadows to look after your horses, you will see a lodge. It will be yours."

The next day it was just as his beloved Black Mare had told him: among his horses there was a lodge, and the mare and her colt were standing beside it. The Black Mare told the man to mix buffalo fat and water, and with charcoal and black clay to paint her on one side of the lodge, and her colt on the other side. "Then paint the night sky at the top," she told him, "with the Seven Stars and the Bunched Stars, and Morning Star at the back. Around the bottom paint a border of red earth hills, and white fallen stars."

When the man had finished painting, the Black Mare led him inside, closed the door, and taught him songs and prayers which he must always remember for as long as he lived in the Horse Lodge. *Fallen stars are painted on the bottom border of many Blackfoot lodges; they are the white puffballs which appear mysteriously overnight among the grass.*

A True Story

This was told to Natalie Curtis by a Winnnebago man as some-one's actual experience when he was a young man, in the late 1800s. Natalie Curtis wrote that the story "gives a deep insight into Indian thought." I present it here, dear Readers and Listeners, as the last story in this book.

There was a young man who was so zealous in his prayers, that he would only be satisfied to dream of *Ma-o-na*, the Earth Maker, God Himself. He would blacken his face, as was the custom to humble oneself, and go to a lonely hilltop where he would fast and pray for many days and nights.

He persevered until he had dreamed of everything in the whole world: the birds and animals, trees, plants, insects, even the smallest spider and ant, but he never saw *Maona*. The Spirits told him: "You have already dreamed of *Maona* because you have dreamed of all His works." But the man was not satisfied, and again he blackened his face, and again he dreamed of the whole world. And then, at last, he dreamed that he heard *Maona*'s voice telling him: "I am Earth Maker. It is not good; you wish for too much. But you will see me tomorrow among the mighty oak trees."

The next morning the man prepared himself and took tobacco for an offering. There, among the tall oaks, the man thought he could see the face of *Maona*, a long face with good eyes. The face spoke to him: "My Son, you have already seen all my works. The Spirits told you this, but you would not believe." The man never turned his eyes away, until at last the vision before him grew dim and drew back its wings; and the man saw it was only a chicken-hawk! He was so sad that he cried and lay down again to dream, but the Spirits came once more and spoke to him: "Stop trying to dream of *Maona*. There are many more birds and animals that may deceive you. Don't try to dream anymore, for you have seen everything."

The man stopped trying to dream of *Maona*. He never saw *Maona*, for no man or woman has ever seen Him. It is not possible to see *Maona*, Earth Maker, God Himself.

If this story seems to contradict the Pawnee story titled "The Man Who Saw the All-Wise-One," it does, but a different people, a different story. . . . Here, in this important and thought-provoking story, Maona *cannot be seen, and anyone who thinks he sees Him is filled with presumption and conceit, and will always be deceived by trivia, like the man deceived by the chicken-hawk. Natalie Curtis concludes: "*Maona *is seen in all his works, and the whole world of nature tells of spiritual life."*